EGMONT

We bring stories to life

This edition published in Great Britain 2011 by Dean,
an imprint of Egmont UK Limited
239 Kensington High Street, London W8 6SA
All rights reserved.

Thomas the Tank Engine & Friends™

HiT entertainment

ISBN 978 0 6035 6618 9
1 3 5 7 9 10 8 6 4 2
Printed in China

Thomas and the Lighthouse

Based on *The Railway Series* by The Rev. W. Awdry

It was the Harvest Festival on the Island of Sodor and everyone was celebrating.

There was to be a big party in the evening.

There would be clowns, the choir would be singing, there would be a fancy dress parade with a Chinese Dragon, and a wonderful firework display!

All the engines had special jobs and they were all very excited – especially Thomas!

The Fat Controller came to Tidmouth Sheds. "Thomas, you must take a new light bulb to the Lighthouse," he said to the little engine.

"Yes, Sir!" Thomas tooted, happily.

The Fat Controller told Thomas that the light bulb had to reach the Lighthouse before dark so that ships at sea could find their way to Sodor safely.

"The light bulb will break easily," The Fat Controller warned Thomas. "You must go slowly and carefully."

So Thomas puffed away to the warehouse.

Thomas collected the light bulb from the warehouse.

Then he set off along the track, moving slowly and carefully, just as The Fat Controller had told him – even though he was very excited about the party.

He slowed at every bend . . .

. . . and chuffed carefully through every junction.

Thomas stopped at a signal. Emily was there.

Emily was excited about the party, too. "The fireworks are going to start when it gets dark," she peeped.

Thomas hoped he would be back in time to see the fireworks. But the Lighthouse was on the far side of the Island of Sodor – a long way away.

An idea flew into Thomas' funnel.

"I'm sure the light bulb won't break if I go just a little faster," he chuffed to himself.

So when the signal changed, Thomas sped up . . . just a little!

At the Water Tower, he saw James, who was pulling trucks full of fireworks.

"This is going to be the biggest firework party ever!" James whistled, happily.

Thomas became even more excited about the fireworks. "I'm sure I can go just a little faster," he chuffed.

He sped up, just a little more.

The bulb began to rattle and shake on Thomas' flatbed trailer.

Just then, Henry huffed past, pulling swings and a seesaw, which were covered with a big sheet.

"It's going to be a wonderful party," puffed Henry.

So Thomas sped up a little more again.

Next, Thomas saw Percy with carriages of children all in fancy dress.

The children were very excited. "See you at the fireworks party, Thomas!" the children called.

Thomas wanted to back for the party more than ever. Before he knew it, he was puffing very fast indeed.

Then there was trouble! Harvey was replacing some tracks.

The workmen had put a barrier across the line.

Thomas was going much too fast to stop safely!

CRASH!

He bashed into the barrier . . .
. . . and the light bulb smashed!

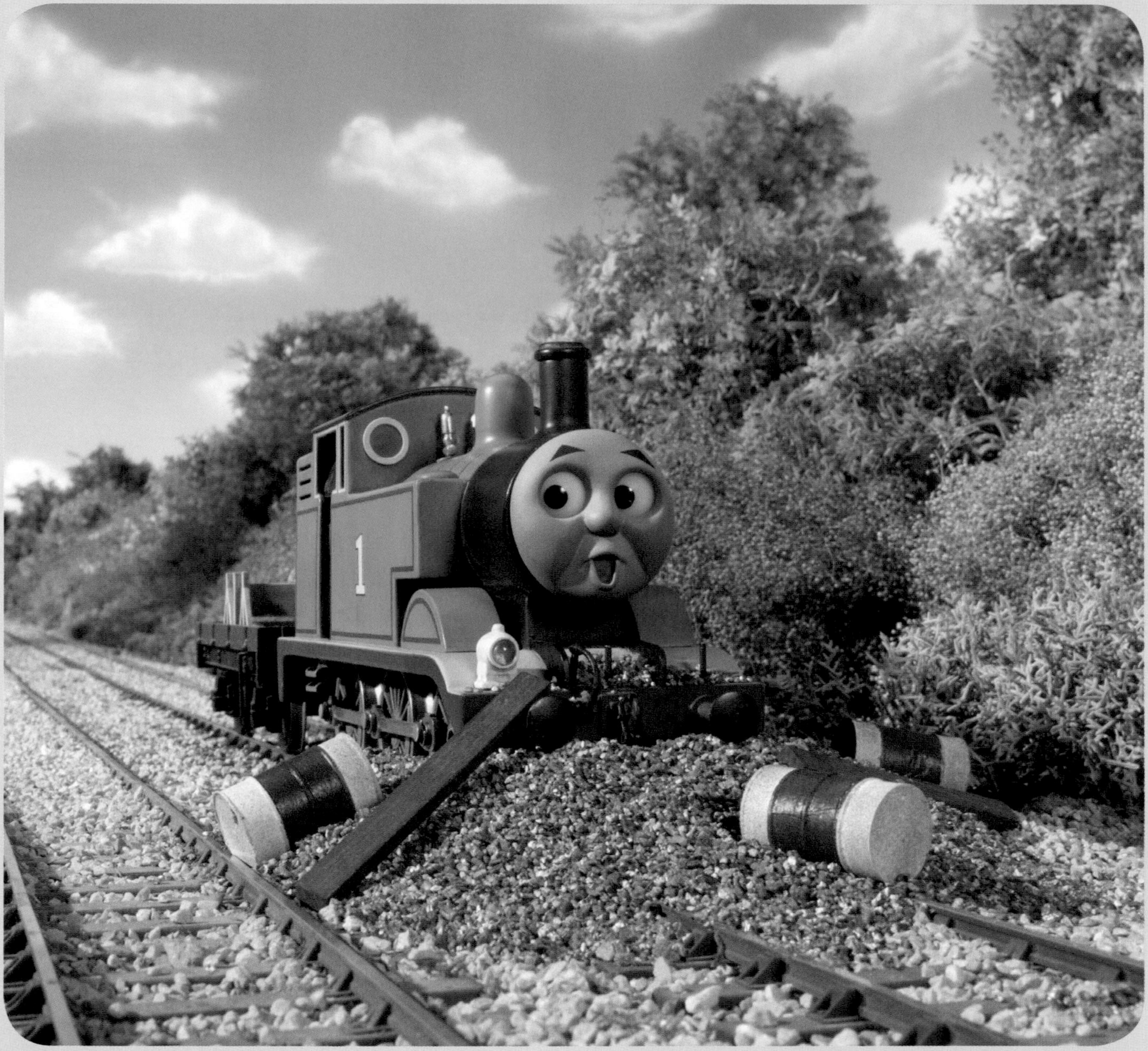
1

"Cinders and ashes!" cried Thomas. "The Lighthouse will not have its light and the sailing ships won't be safe at sea!"

Thomas knew what he had to do.

He puffed back to the warehouse to collect a new light bulb as fast as his wheels would carry him.

Now Thomas knew he would be back too late to see the fireworks.

On the way, Thomas stopped at the signal.

Gordon was waiting there and he was very excited. "I'm off to collect the Chinese Dragon," he tooted, happily.

But all Thomas could think about was fetching the new light bulb.

He tried not to think about the party he was going to miss.

Thomas returned to the warehouse.

The new light bulb was placed gently on his flatbed and Thomas set off along the track again – slowly and carefully.

Toby passed him with the choir, who were practising their songs.

Then Edward passed him, proudly pulling the Chinese Dragon.

But Thomas didn't think about the firework party once! He had an important job to do.

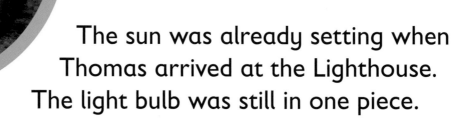

The sun was already setting when Thomas arrived at the Lighthouse. The light bulb was still in one piece.

"Thank you, Thomas," said the lighthouse keeper, as the bulb was unloaded from Thomas' flatbed.

Thomas puffed back to Tidmouth Sheds. He knew he had missed the fireworks.

He was very disappointed.

But when Thomas came to the top of a hill he saw a brilliant sight.

The Lighthouse beam shone brightly, the ships' lights twinkled in the Harbour and the stars were reflected in the sea.

Thomas thought that all the lights looked just as wonderful as fireworks!